SUPER HAPPY PARTY BEARS

BAT TO THE BONE

BAT TO THE BONE

MARCIE COLLEEN

[Imprint]
MAKE YOUR MARK
NEW YORK

☺ ☻ ☹ ☻ 😍 **[Imprint]** 😮 😣 😦 ☺ 😃
MAKE YOUR MARK

A part of Macmillan Children's Publishing Group,
a division of Macmillan Publishing Group, LLC

Library of Congress Control Number: 2016954108
ISBN 978-1-250-11357-3 (paperback) / ISBN 978-1-250-11356-6 (ebook)
Our books may be purchased in bulk for promotional, educational,
or business use. Please contact your local bookseller or the Macmillan
Corporate and Premium Sales Department at (800) 221-7945 ext. 5442
or by e-mail at MacmillanSpecialMarkets@macmillan.com.

Book design by Christine Kell
Imprint logo designed by Amanda Spielman
Illustrations by Steve James

First Edition—2017

1 3 5 7 9 10 8 6 4 2

mackids.com

😐

If this isn't your book, keep your thieving paws off it.
Obey or may every piñata you break be filled with broccoli.

TO MY BFF. STEPH.
THIRTY YEARS AND COUNTING!

CHAPTER ONE

Welcome to the Grumpy Woods!

Now turn around, and don't let that tree branch hit you on the way out.

That's right. Turn around and keep walking, or Sheriff Sherry

1

will haul you off to City Hall. No
exceptions.

No one is welcome here.

You see, everyone is still reeling
from the latest incident. A bunch
of chipmunks and squirrels had

a major rumble on the Grumpy
Grassland, and the ground caved
in! It was a disaster. True, they
found a cave filled with nutty
treasure, but it was still a disaster!

Mayor Quill held a very official

meeting at City Hall. Everyone—
from Bernice Bunny to Opal Owl—
attended. Except the Super Happy
Party Bears. They weren't invited,
because no one was in the mood
for doughnuts and dancing.

Right now you are probably

thinking *Yum, doughnuts* and *Who doesn't like to bust a move?* Well, the Grumpy townscritters, that's who!

At this particular town meeting, it was decided that something needed to be done to reconstruct

the Grumpy Grassland. All the nuts
once stored there had been eaten,
so it was just an empty ditch.

One too many townscritters had
fallen into the hole while passing
through the woods. The worst
was when Bernice Bunny, hopping
around with her nose in a book,

tumbled right in! She was stuck
there until Dawn Fawn found her
and pulled her out by lowering
her feather duster into the crater
and having Bernice hang on. The
rescue was joyous until Dawn Fawn
wouldn't let Bernice go and used
her as her "dust bunny" for the rest

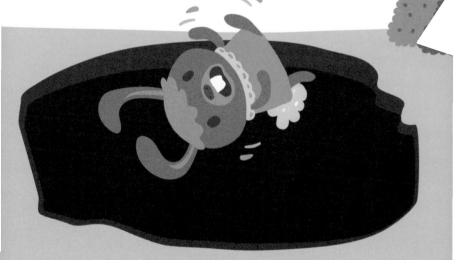

of the day. Right then and there, Bernice decided to lead the fight to "Ditch the Ditch."

Everyone voted. And that was that. It was very official. But the question was *how* to fill in the pit.

Humphrey Hedgehog, assistant deputy to Mayor Quill, presented his blueprints for a state-of-the-art

Ditch
the
Ditch

9

swimming pool, complete with
twisty slide and diving board. The
mayor shot down that idea because
there was already a members-only
watering hole (of which he was the

only member), so he didn't see the need for a swimming pool.

Squirrelly Sam proposed refilling the crater with nuts. Apparently, he'd forgotten that the rumble was all about nuts in the first place.

Sheriff Sherry suggested turning the hole into a sandbox. She loved to build sand castles. But Dawn

Fawn pointed out that sand might attract beach animals. And she thought seagulls were the dirtiest of birds.

Finally, they decided to simply fill the ditch with dirt and rename it the Grumpy Flats.

Everyone grabbed a shovel. Everyone complained. And everyone got a backache after only a few shovelfuls. But it was the first time the townscritters had ever worked together and succeeded. They are pretty proud

of their teamwork. But they are still grumpy.

And so, every day, everyone in the Grumpy Woods wakes up with a crick in their neck and orders up some breakfast—a small bowl of Cranky Flakes and a side order of *puh-leeze*.

That is, everyone except the Super Happy Party Bears.

Welcome to PARTY PATCH

If you travel just beyond the new Grumpy Flats and follow the carefully placed sticks, laid out in the shape of arrows, up the flower-lined path, you'll see a welcome sign. That's the Party Patch, the Headquarters of Fun. Life there is very different.

Life is super. Life is happy.

LIFE IS FULL OF PARTIES!

And so, on any beautiful morning, the Super Happy Party Bears bounce out of bed and order up some breakfast—a slice of pie-eating grins topped with *goody-goody gumdrops*!

Nothing annoys their Grumpy
Woods neighbors more.

Except when the bears have a
party.

And they are always having a
party.

CHAPTER TWO

The moon rose high over the Grumpy Woods. Over at the Party Patch, the Headquarters of Fun, a Super Happy Bedtime Party was in full swing.

CRUNCH–CRUNCH–GULP!

The bears ate their bedtime snacks: doughnut holes and warm milk with marshmallows.

Jigs took a long sip of her milk. "Look at my mustache!"

Soon everyone had a milk mustache and ate the rest of their snack while speaking with funny stuffy accents.

"Mops, dear sir, would you be kind enough to pass another marshmallow?" asked Shades.

"Why, of course, good sir!" Mops, with pinkie finger out to the side, passed the marshmallow daintily to Shades.

The littlest bear, done with being all prim and proper, announced, "Who wants to play One Million Marshmallows?

"On your mark! Get set! Go!"

All the bears stuffed their cheeks with marshmallows and then tried to say "one million marshmallows" clearly.

"Wub willion washwallows," said Little Puff.

"Murthuhmphumph," said Flips, covering his mouth to keep the marshmallows in.

"One. Million. Marsh. Mallows,"
said Bubs. He was clearly at
an advantage. His cheeks were
in tip-top shape from all the
bubble-blowing.

Next, the bears lined up at the
sink, one behind the other, to brush
their teeth.

Scritch-scritch swish-swish spit!

And then they raced to put on
their footy pajamas—*Zip-zip-snap!*

Finally, no Super Happy Bedtime
Party would be complete without a
pillow fight.

Whip-whip-smack!

Once the last pillow feathers floated to the ground, the littlest bear struggled under the weight of a stack of books.

"Story time," he announced.

"Remember Quilly's decree!" said Jacks. He was referring to Mayoral Decree 2,322: Two books and lights-out!

The littlest bear reluctantly put the extra books back and made sure to read only two.

The bears snuggled together in a big rainbow-colored pile.

Ziggy played one last song of the day on his guitar. *Strum-strum-lull.* Every furry eyelid drooped, and the bears were off to dreamland.

The littlest bear's legs twitched as he dreamed of dancing, while

Big Puff's faint snores seemed to keep rhythm to "If You're Happy and You Know It."

The Party Patch was quiet.

No doughnuts, no music, no cheering, and certainly no more parties . . . until breakfast.

CHAPTER THREE

This was Opal Owl's time of day...
er, night.

She poured herself another cup
of acorn tea, propped up her fuzzy-
slippered feet, and got to work on
her latest jigsaw puzzle—a photo
of a cranky platypus saying, "If you

are looking for bright-eyed and bushy-tailed, go find a squirrel."

Opal was working on completing the platypus's tail.

She chuckled. "I might just have to glue you together and place you on the wall when I am finished."

Around her treehouse Opal displayed several glued-together puzzles that she thought were "too cute" or "too funny" to take apart. There was barely room for another, except on the wall where she had proudly hung the macramé owl made by her nephew, Blink. He had crafted it in Owlet Scouts.

Opal took a sip of her acorn tea and smiled as she thought of her sweet nephew. He would be coming to visit his auntie Opal soon, as he did every year. Opal looked

forward to their nighttime hunts.
They always had such a hoot
enjoying the Grumpy Woods when
everyone else was asleep. Being
the only nocturnal townscritter
sure had its perks.

Suddenly, Opal's memories
were interrupted by a low

BOOM, followed by a screechy

REEN-
REEN-REEN.

The cranky platypus shifted,

causing his tail to break from

the rest of the puzzle. Opal's tea

rippled in its mug. The macramé

owl trembled, its beady eyes

clicking against the wall.

"What in the world?" said Opal, stooping to pick up some puzzle pieces that had fallen onto the floor.

BOOM! once again. And then a faint squealing *REEN-REEN-REEN*.

Opal shuffled to the window and squinted at the woods below. It was dark, but Opal's extraordinary night vision enabled her to see clearly. She saw nothing.

"Must have been the wind,"
she tried to convince herself.
After all, no other townscritter
could see in the dark without a
flashlight. And Humphrey Hedgehog
hadn't been sleepwalking, or
Opal would have heard the
TINKLE-TINKLE-TINKLE
of the bell that Mayor Quill had
officially decreed he wear around
his neck ever since the night the
mayor's teddy bear, Senator Fluffy,
went missing and was later found
in Humphrey's bed. No one was

sure which was worse: learning
that the mayor had named his
teddy bear Senator Fluffy or
hearing the mayor scream like a
little porcupette when the bear
went missing.

But just as Opal settled back down, there came another *BOOM! BOOM!* and *REEN-REEN-WAAAHHHHH!* This one was louder and seemed to vibrate longer. Opal jumped,

spilling the mug of acorn tea all over the puzzle. The macramé owl gave a shudder and slipped off the wall. One of its beady eyes came loose and rolled across the floor.

It sounded like Ziggy's guitar.

AAHHHHH!

CHAPTER FOUR

With the macramé owl's beady
eye clutched in her talons, Opal
swooped into City Hall. A town
meeting was already in progress.
Everyone was there and wide
awake. Even Senator Fluffy was
propped up on the podium.

Humphrey Hedgehog, in his fancy pajamas with the jingly bell hanging from the zipper, clamored to calm the crowd but was failing miserably.

"We assure you that we are looking into the cause of this horrible noise as I speak," said Humphrey. "Sheriff Sherry is already out investigating."

"You didn't hear this from me," said Squirrelly Sam, "but the only thing Sherry is investigating right now is the back of her eyelids."

"Sssss . . . sssss . . . sssss." Sherry was coiled up and snoring in the back of the room.

"LULLABY AND GOOD NIGHT! LULLABY AND GOOD NIGHT!"

Dawn Fawn sang out hysterically,
still gripping her pillow.

"Two books and lights-out!
It's been decreed!" cried Bernice
Bunny. Of course, that particular
decree was not always followed by

Bernice herself. But silently reading under her covers with a flashlight never bothered anyone. She held quite a grudge against the Super Happy Party Bears for causing the decree in the first place.

"The list of culprits to investigate is short," said Humphrey Hedgehog, holding up his clipboard.

"Excuse me," said Squirrelly Sam, "but what if it isn't

possible culprits
1. The Super Happy Party Bears

the bears this time? What if it's monsters?"

"There are no monsters in the Grumpy Woods," said Quill.

"M-m-m-monsters?" sang Dawn, anxiously humming and rocking back and forth.

"Really, Sam, this isn't helping," harrumphed Humphrey. "It's just the bears."

"But maybe the bears turned into Super Happy Party Zombies and are roaming the woods looking for us." Bernice's fuzzy ears

trembled. "I read a book about
that."

"Makes sense," said Mayor Quill,
pulling Senator Fluffy closer. "That
last boom-boom did kind of sound
like gigantic furry feet."

"Oh my goodness," whispered

Sam. "I bet it's the ghost of One-Tail Willy. He's looking for his stolen stash of nuts. I didn't do it! I didn't do it!" Sam skittered in circles,

47

finally grabbing his tail and hiding behind it.

"Enough of this!" said Humphrey. "Maybe it's just the bears having a party. Ever think of that?"

The other townscritters stared blankly at Humphrey.

"The mayor and I will head to the Party Patch to investigate—" started Humphrey.

"I'm not going to that den of ginormous monsters!" protested Mayor Quill.

49

"Well, someone has to go," said
Humphrey.

Just then, another *BOOM!*
BOOM! REEN-REEN-WAAAHHHHH!
thundered. Humphrey rolled into
a shivering defensive ball. Sam

REEN~REEN~
WAAAHHHHH!

jumped and scurried up Dawn's legs, burying his face in her fur. Sherry sprang awake and coiled up into a ball, while Mayor Quill and Senator Fluffy snuggled for survival.

"I hear feet," whispered Sam.

"Would ghossssstssss have feet?" hiss-pered Sherry.

"Zombie Bear Ghosts would," said Sam. "Big, furry ones."

"I can't look!" sang Dawn, hiding her head in her pillow.

But as frightened as they all were, the townscritters were also quite curious. They sneakily peeked out the window and saw a shuffling crowd of intimidating-looking animals pass right by City Hall.

52

"Nocturnals," whispered Humphrey.

Opal huffed. The term *nocturnals* was not a kind one, and definitely not a label Opal liked.

"Where do you think they are headed?" asked Mayor Quill.

But before anyone could answer, a loud hammering noise came from the tallest tree in the woods. The tree where all Mayoral Decrees were posted.

"What are those ruffians doing to my tree?" shrieked Mayor Quill, and he burst out the door to investigate. The townscritters followed. But it was too late.

The Mayoral Decrees were still there. However, they were completely covered up with some sort of advertisement.

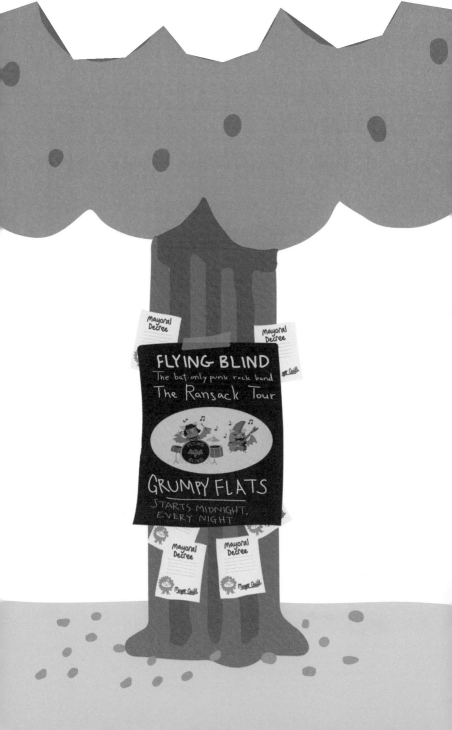

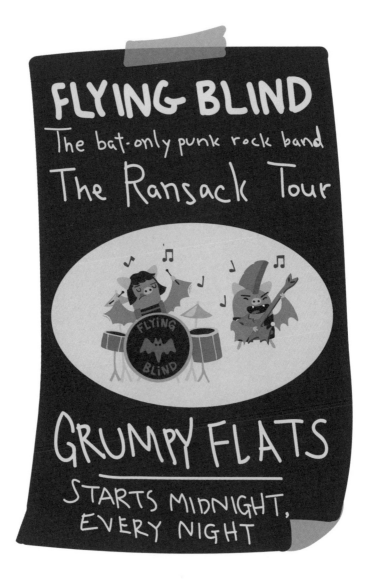

FLYING BLIND

The bat-only punk rock band

The Ransack Tour

GRUMPY FLATS

STARTS MIDNIGHT, EVERY NIGHT

A bat wearing a leather jacket with chains zigged up to Dawn Fawn. "Tickets? Anyone need tickets?"

Dawn slowly shook her head.

"Your loss. It's gonna be so

totally sonar, dude," said the bat, and he high-fived a raccoon.

"They've already started the sound check," said the raccoon, and he scurried off.

"Keep moving, day dweller," said a mouse with a Mohawk that was almost double his height. For a little creature, he was quite loud.

Sherry hissed at the mouse and showed her badge. When the mouse had no reaction, she bared her fangs instead.

A gray cat with enormous eyes

and a shock of red-dyed hair slunk

between Sherry and the mouse.

"Vermin, stop picking fights.

Tonight is about the meeee-usic."

To Sherry, she added, "Sorry about that. Vermin's a little guy with a big attitude. He'll simmer down once the concert starts."

"MOSH PIT!" yelled a honey badger, and the crowd hollered and pushed forward faster. The townscritters stumbled as they were caught in the frenzy.

Mayor Quill had had enough of this nonsense. He stomped his foot. He shook from head to toe. Just before the mayor exploded, the townscritters took cover.

Quills flew everywhere. One soared through the pack and speared Vermin's Mohawk.

Everyone stopped and looked at the townscritters.

After a moment of silence, the mob erupted into roaring applause and chanted, "*Spike! Spike! Spike!*" as they continued on toward the concert.

"My name is not Spike!" yelled Mayor Quill.

"Let's get out of here, Spike—er, I mean, sir," said Humphrey, and the townscritters scampered back to City Hall.

CHAPTER FIVE

Mayor Quill headed straight to
his office and collapsed in his
chair. He wasn't used to so much
excitement way past his bedtime.
All the other townscritters
huddled around him, eager to hear

how the mayor planned to take
care of this newest crisis.

Mayor Quill plucked a fresh quill
from his backside. He dipped it
carefully in his inkpot.

Mayoral Decree

2,500.1

There are to be no punk rock concerts or music concerts of any kind in the Grumpy Woods.

Mayor Quill

Mayoral Decree

2,500.2

Nocturnals except Opal Owl are bad news and should be kicked out of the Grumpy Woods.

Mayor Quill

Mayor Decree
2,500.3
Do not call the mayor "Spike." Ever!

Mayor Quill

He underlined that last point not once, not twice, but five times. The mayor wasn't messing around. Then he stood to read the decrees aloud

in his "I am the mayor and everyone
needs to listen to me" voice.

"I hereby declare, by order of—"

Sam interrupted. "You didn't

hear this from me, but everyone already read the decrees over your shoulder."

The rest of the townscritters agreed. They were all grumpier than usual. Grumpy and exhausted equaled cranky beyond belief!

"It's true, sir," said Humphrey. "We can probably just move on to the part where we take action."

"Well then," said the mayor, "Opal Owl needs to negotiate on our behalf and tell all those concert-going hoodlums they need

to leave the Grumpy Woods this instant."

"They'll listen to you," said Bernice to Opal Owl. "You are one of them."

"I am nothing like those hoOOOodlums," said Opal.

"You know what we mean,"

said Humphrey. "A nocturnal." He whispered the last part like it was a bad thing to say. Opal just glared at him and turned her head to face the other way.

"Pleasssse, Opal," said Sherry. "The ssssooner you do thissss, the ssssooner we'll go to ssssleep and give you back the night."

"Otherwise we'll all just have to live like nocturnals," said Mayor Quill.

"And think about Blink. You don't want him exposed to these ruffians when he comes to visit in a few weeks, do you?" asked Sam.

Opal could feel the pleading eyes of each townscritter on the back of her head. They had a point. She was not about to share her nights with day dwellers. And Blink—he was such an innocent little owlet.

"Fine," agreed Opal.

"Totally sonar!" said Humphrey. The others glared at him, so he quickly added, "I guess we can be happy about one thing. The Super Happy Party Bears are sound asleep. We'll have this all taken care of by morning, and they will eat their doughnuts never even having known that any of this happened."

Just then, a conga line of rainbow-colored bears paraded by City Hall.

"WE LOVE ROCK 'N' ROLL!" cheered the bears.

CHAPTER SIX

Let's back up for a second.

You see, while the townscritters were worrying about Super Happy Party Zombies and mosh pits, the *BOOM! BOOM! REEN-REEN-WAHHH!* sound check rattled the welcome-mat roof of the Party Patch.

One of the Flying Blind concert flyers came sliding underneath the bear-shaped door and landed right in front of Mops's nose. He opened one eye, read it, and then—

"SUPER HAPPY CONCERT TIME!"

he announced.

Faster than you can say

doughnut, the bears popped up

from their sleepy heap.

"SUPER HAPPY CONCERT TIME!

SUPER HAPPY CONCERT TIME!"

the bears chanted, and did their

Super Happy Party Dance right out

of their pajamas.

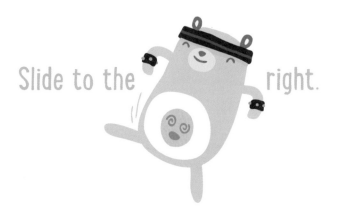

Slide to the   right.

Hop to the left.

Shimmy, shimmy, shake.

Strike a pose.

79

"Preparation," Bubs said,

opening a fresh bottle of bubbles,

"is the key to any party's success."

Within seconds they had conga-

lined out the door.

"WE LOVE ROCK 'N' ROLL!"

cheered the bears as they danced

past City Hall and met up with

the crowd of fans heading to the
Grumpy Flats.

"So do I," commented the gray
cat with the shock of red-dyed hair,
"but this crowd is crazy. Follow
me."

She gracefully zipped through
the crowd like juice through a

twisty straw. The bears bounced along behind. Finally, they arrived at a roped-off area in front of a colossal stage that was draped in cobweb decorations and surrounded by speakers as big as the Party Patch. In the center of the stage, bathed in pale blue spotlights, were a sparkling red drum kit and an equally shiny electric guitar.

"Welcome to the Bat Cave. Home to the biggest fans of Flying Blind," said the cat. "Let me introduce you.

First, I'm Josie, but all my friends call me Miss Pounce." She held out her paw but then promptly licked it.

The littlest bear giggled and
licked his paw, too. "Tastes like
powdered sugar!"

"I think you've met Vermin."
The Mohawked mouse ignored the
introduction.

"This is Grabby." A raccoon in
the corner waved to the bears.

In her hands were a pair of star glasses and one of Jigs's maracas.

"I have glasses just like that," said Shades, suddenly wondering where his glasses had gone. Jigs shook one maraca and laughed.

"Hold on to your belongings. She takes everything!" warned Miss Pounce.

Just then, a large honey badger lumbered by. He was wearing a Flying Blind T-shirt and carrying an armload of snacks.

"Randall, you're making a mess!" said Vermin.

"I DON'T CARE!" yelled Randall, plopping down in front for the best view of the stage.

"Randall doesn't care about anything," explained Miss Pounce. "It's better if you just leave him alone. He's a honey badger with the emphasis on *bad*."

"How long have you been fans of Flying Blind?" asked Grabby, who was suddenly wearing Jacks's sweatband.

"Since we woke up about five minutes ago," said Tunes.

"ARE YOU READY TO GET TOTALLY SONAR?!" boomed a

voice on the speakers. The crowd, including the bears, went wild. "PUT YOUR WINGS AND PAWS TOGETHER FOR FLYING BLIND!"

The pale blue spotlight went out, and colored lights swirled around the stage.

Suddenly...

BOOM!

BOOM!

REEN~REEN~

WAAAHHHH!

Two bats jammed out on their instruments. The one on guitar was screaming into a microphone.

"Ransack!

Snack attack!

Open up that trash can—

just a crack!"

It was very different from the music the bears were used to, but they were instant fans.

CHAPTER SEVEN

Once again, Opal cut through the night air on a mission: to convince Flying Blind to leave the Grumpy Woods so that the townscritters could get back to sleep and she could get on with her life of solitude.

She circled twice above the concert to plan her strategy. The ground seemed to be bouncing to the rhythm of the music. By now hundreds of fans, all wearing red and black in support of Flying Blind, had gathered, and the

Grumpy Flats was a massive mosh pit. A cloud of bats formed like a wave and tossed other fans to and fro. A honey badger surfed the crowd, howling as he was passed from fan to fan. And then a rainbow burst forth as a dozen bears joined in the crowd-surfing, giggling all the way.

"Surfing tickles!" shouted the littlest bear over the music.

"HoOOOoligans, every one of them," said Opal, rolling her big yellow eyes. Sam was right: She needed to put a stop to this before Blink arrived in a few weeks.

And that's when Opal saw him, climbing up from the mosh pit. "Blink!"

Her poor nephew! He must have been kidnapped by these louts.

Blink stood at the center of the stage, in front of the musicians, with his wings outstretched. He was wearing a Flying Blind T-shirt.

"BLINK! BLINK! BLINK!"

the crowd chanted, and the boy
owl skyrocketed off the stage and
buzzed across the tops of heads.
Fans below reached up to him with
outstretched arms.

Opal immediately dove in front
of Blink.

97

"Auntie Opal?!" said the startled owl. "I didn't know you listened to this stuff."

Opal's eyes were angry and squinty. She grabbed the tip of Blink's wing and tugged him over to a branch.

"Are you okay?" Opal asked. "Are these ruffians holding you captive? Because that is about the only explanation I will accept right now."

"No way, Auntie Opal. This stuff is totally sonar. All the cool kids are listening to it. That's why I'm

spending my summer following the

Flying Blind tour. You know, I'm not

an owlet anymore."

From the stage, the lead singer

announced the next song. "This

one is called 'Rabid Rhapsody.'"

"That's my song!" said Blink.

And without even a peck on the cheek, he disappeared into the crowd, leaving Opal alone with only her macramé-owl's beady eye and memories.

CHAPTER EIGHT

Opal returned to City Hall while the concert raged on.

"What do you mean, you didn't talk to them?" asked Mayor Quill. "You had a very official job to do."

Opal buried her face in her wings. Between sobs she managed

to tell the others that she had seen
Blink. That he was different. That
he was now "one of them."

"You didn't hear this from me,"
said Sam, "but Blink always seemed
a bit *rock 'n' roll* to me."

Opal lifted her face long enough
to throw a scowl in Sam's direction,
and then she flew out of the room
to be alone.

"Sssssomething sssstill needssss
to be done," said Sherry. "The
crowd issss out of control. I can't
handle ssssuch a large ruckussss."

*BOOM! BOOM! REEN-REEN-
WAAAHHHHH!*

"If only that noise had an off
switch!" griped Mayor Quill.

"That's it, sir!" said Humphrey.
"We'll march down there and

unplug their sound equipment.

That'll stop them."

"Won't they just plug it all back in?" asked Sam.

"Not if we gnaw the cords so they can't be used again," explained Humphrey.

"I am *not* gnawing electrical

cords," said Bernice. "We'll get electrocuted."

"We unplug them firsssst, ssssilly," said Sherry.

"But without Opal, how will we see where we are going?" asked Sam.

"This large box of Flying Blind merchandise arrived for Spike— er, I mean, the mayor." Humphrey passed out glow sticks and blinking necklaces. "These things will help us see in the dark. I don't think he will mind if we wear them."

Mayor Quill snorted in disgust. "By order of Mayoral Decree number two thousand five hundred point three—" he started.

"We know, we know. Do not call the mayor 'Spike.' Ever!" finished the townscritters as they put on the accessories.

When Humphrey thought no one
was watching, he also slipped on
a Flying Blind T-shirt. He caught a
puzzled look from Dawn, and he
quickly said, "We have to blend in.
It's my disguise."

So, decked out in glowing gear,

the townscritters headed for the Grumpy Flats. Everyone grumbled about it, but no one had a better idea.

Once at the concert, those with the sharpest teeth—Sam, Bernice, and Sherry—headed to the power outlets to unplug the sound system and gnaw on the cords. Humphrey, the mayor, and Dawn acted as lookouts from the bushes.

While hiding, Humphrey felt a tug on the bottom of his Flying Blind T-shirt. He turned to see the littlest

bear, who was wearing sunglasses

and looked slightly more punk than

usual.

"Excuse me, Mr. Humphrey, I like your glowing necklace," yelled the littlest bear over the music. "Would you like some glasses? They help you appreciate the music more."

"Oooh," said Humphrey, "I don't mind if I do."

"We do not want any glasses!" interrupted Mayor Quill. "And we do *not* want to appreciate this *music*, or whatever it is called." He stomped his foot. He shook from head to toe.

"Deep breaths, sir," said

Humphrey. "We don't want to draw any unnecessary attention." As Mayor Quill closed his eyes and tried to calm down, Humphrey snuck a pair of glasses and winked at the littlest bear.

Just then, the music stopped. Flying Blind was silenced. Luna's drums barely boomed. And without its electricity, Echo's guitar ceased to *reen-reen*.

"Yes!" said Mayor Quill triumphantly. "Operation Gnaw is complete."

Sam, Bernice, and Sherry quickly joined the others in the bushes. They high-fived when they saw one another. In fact, they even cheered a little bit. Lack of sleep can make townscritters do things they wouldn't normally do.

The crowd booed and tossed snacks at the stage. Dawn covered her eyes to avoid seeing the mess.

Mayor Quill chuckled. "Come on, Senator Fluffy. It sounds like bedtime to me."

But Flips appeared on the stage, using his hat as a megaphone. "We apologize for the mishap. Are you still ready to rock?" The crowd cheered.

A drumstick poked Flips from behind. "What are you doing?" whispered Luna through clenched teeth.

"We don't have any juice. This gig is over," said Echo, putting down his guitar.

Then the Super Happy Party Band appeared onstage, pushing their own amplifier.

"Have no fear," said Flips.

His voice boomed from the new system. "This one goes all the way to eleven."

The crowd exploded in applause. "Bears! Bears! Bears! Bears!"

Ziggy handed his guitar to Echo, and Big Puff gave one of his drumsticks to Luna.

"Let's get happy!" yelled Ziggy.

"One! Two! Three! Four!" Big Puff and Luna hit the drumsticks together, and the music started once again.

Echo sang out, "Ransack! Snack attack!"

Ziggy joined in. "If you're happy and you know it, eat that snack!"

CHAPTER NINE

The bands jammed as if two radio stations were playing at the same time. The dark and angry Flying Blind music collided with the incredibly cheerful Super Happy Party Band. Imagine what a super-fast merry-go-round would sound

like if it spun backward. Throw in some giggles and angry yelling, and that's what the music mash-up sounded like.

The townscritters were grumpier than ever. The Super Happy Party Bears had once again ruined their plan, and they were fresh out of ideas.

119

"Make it stop!" whimpered Bernice.

"This has been the longest night ever!" whined Sam.

"I can't think with all this racket!" Mayor Quill buried his face in Senator Fluffy's belly. "Where's the sun when you need it?"

"That's it!" said Humphrey. "We'll make it morning so that all the nocturnals will go to bed."

"Ssssure. We'll jusssst assssk the ssssun to sssshine," snapped Sherry.

"We don't need the sun." Humphrey pointed to the giant towers of lights that surrounded the Grumpy Flats. They were currently flashing an array of color onto the stage. But a simple flip of a switch could change the light to bright white.

"Humphrey," said Mayor Quill, "I am so tired, I could kiss you."

The encore of "Ransack! Snack Attack!" lasted fifteen minutes. Mostly it was so long because each bear wanted to have their own dance break.

"Go, Flips! It's your birthday! We're gonna party like it's your birthday!"

Echo and Luna exchanged looks
when they realized there were a
dozen bears.

When the bears were finally
finished, Flying Blind attempted to
gain back control.

"This next song is called 'Get
Outta My Belfry,'" announced
Echo. Then to the Super Happy

Party Band, he added, "Just follow me. It's a repeated D and G chord progression."

"Righty-o," said Ziggy.

"We cats got ya covered," said Big Puff.

Of course, the Super Happy Party Band played "If You're Happy and You Know It." Again.

"This music stinks!" yelled
Vermin from the ground below.

"I'm outta here," said Grabby,
her arms full of Flying Blind
merchandise.

"It's always sad when a band
sells out," said Miss Pounce.

"I DON'T CARE ANYMORE!"

Randall screamed at the stage. Then he turned to leave, too.

"Hey!" said Echo. "Where's everyone going?"

"No worries," said Little Puff. "We're still here."

"I might be blind," said Luna, "but I know a dead-end gig when I see one."

"Sorry, bears," said Echo. "You just aren't punk rock enough."

Just then, a flood of white light illuminated the Grumpy Flats.

"Mwah-ha-ha!" Mayor Quill's laughter echoed across the field. "Take that, you pestering nocturnals!"

But the Grumpy Flats were empty. The crowd was gone. All that remained were a few dancing bears.

"I don't understand," said Humphrey, rubbing his tired eyes.

"Sorry, dude. You can thank

those annoying bears," said Echo, wrapped in his wings to shield himself from the light.

"Concert's over," said Luna.

"We'll rock it in the next town," said Ziggy.

"*We* will. Don't follow us," said Echo, and Flying Blind flew off into the shadows.

Meanwhile, the townscritters looked over the Grumpy Flats. There was trash everywhere.

"CLEAN UP! CLEAN UP!" sang Dawn.

"Look at what those ruffians did to our flats," said Humphrey. "It'll take all night to clean up."

"Not if we work together," came a voice from behind him. It was Blink. And he was holding several trash bags. "I take my 'Don't Litter' Owlet Scouts badge seriously!"

"Blink!" Opal Owl swooped down and hugged her nephew.

"Auntie Opal," said Blink, "can I stay here this summer? Seems the tour is moving on without me."

"YoOOOu betcha," said Opal.

Together, the townscritters and the bears cleaned up the Grumpy Flats in no time at all. It's a wonder what can be accomplished with a little teamwork.

The sun started to rise. Everyone was exhausted after having stayed up all night.

"I decree it's time for bed," announced Mayor Quill.

"But first we need to have a snack, play One Million Marshmallows, zip into our pajamas, brush our teeth, have a pillow fight, and then two books and lights-out," said the littlest bear.

"What is One Million

Marshmallows?" asked Humphrey.

"We'll show you," said Mops.

"SUPER HAPPY BEDTIME PARTY!
SUPER HAPPY BEDTIME PARTY!"

cheered the bears.

And you know what?

The townscritters cheered, too.

They were feeling just a *little* less
grumpy. THE END.

ABOUT THE AUTHOR

In previous chapters, Marcie Colleen has been a teacher, an actress, and a nanny, but now she spends her days writing children's books! She lives in her very own Party Patch, Headquarters of Fun, with her husband and their mischievous sock monkey in San Diego, California. Occasionally, there are even doughnuts. This is her first chapter book series.